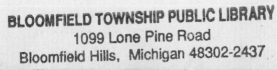

BIG BROTHER MIKE

BIG BROTHER MIKE

DAN YACCARINO

Hyperion Books for Children
New York

For more information address Hyperion Books for Children,
114 Fifth Avenue, New York, New York 10011.

First Edition
1 3 5 7 9 10 8 6 2

Library of Congress Cataloging-in-Publication Data
Yaccarino, Dan.
Big brother Mike / Dan Yaccarino—1st ed.
p. cm.
Summary: A young boy tells why he thinks his big brother
Mike doesn't like him, but then he remembers some
of the nice things Mike has done for him.
ISBN 1-56282-329-9 (trade)—ISBN 1-56282-330-2 (lib. bdg.)
[1. Brothers—Fiction.] I. Title.
PZ7.Y125Bi 1993 [E]—dc20 92-72017 CIP AC

The art for each picture consists of gouache painted on
Arches coldpress watercolor paper.

To Mom, Dad, Susie, and, of course,
my big brother Mike

I just know my big brother Mike doesn't like me.

Soon after I was born he asked Mom, "Can you take him back now?"

And when she said no, he tried to mail me.

He always gets to the cereal box first,

and he likes my toys better than his.

When we watch TV,
he calls himself
Master Controller.

The day his drum broke, he used me instead.

And when we play "rescue," I'm always the victim.

At the playground he pushes me too high on the swings,

he never lets me down on the seesaw,

and he makes the whirl-around spin too fast.

My big brother Mike is NEVER nice to me . . . .

Well, *almost* never.

There *was* the morning he helped me bury my hamster when it died.

When some older kids laughed and called me a baby,

he told me it was alright to cry.

After lunch, we built a fort.

Then he let me clean out his bird's cage,

and that night *I* was Master Controller!

You know what?
I think my big brother Mike likes me after all.